THE ADVENTURES OF PINOCCHIO™

Adapted by M.J. Carr
From the screenplay by Sherry Mills & Steve Barron and Barry Berman

SCHOLASTIC INC.
New York Toronto London Auckland Sydney

ISBN 0-590-92263-7

Text copyright © 1996 by
The Kushner-Locke Company/Savoy Pictures, Inc./New Line Productions, Inc. All rights reserved.
Artwork copyright © 1995 by The Kushner-Locke Company. All rights reserved.
Published by Scholastic Inc.
CARLO COLLODI'S PINOCCHIO is a trademark of The Kushner-Locke Company.

12 11 10 9 8 7 6 5 4 3 2 1   6 7 8 9/9 0 1/0

Printed in the U.S.A.   24

First Scholastic printing, August 1996

In a little town in Italy that was tucked into the edge of a great pine forest, there once lived a man named Geppetto. Geppetto was a woodsman. Each day, he trudged into the forest to cut wood for the people of the town. Sometimes he found oddly shaped, unusual pieces. He put them aside to carve into puppets, for Geppetto was a craftsman as well.

One day, a log rolled in front of Geppetto's cart. Geppetto studied the wood. It was rough and weathered. Though Geppetto did not notice, under the bark was a heart he had once carved into the tree. Geppetto took the log home. He could carve it into a beautiful wooden boy.

Geppetto carved the wood into a puppet. He chiseled wide, innocent eyes, and whittled a branch into a nose.

"You are made of pine and you have beautiful eyes," said Geppetto. "Your name will be Pinocchio."

5

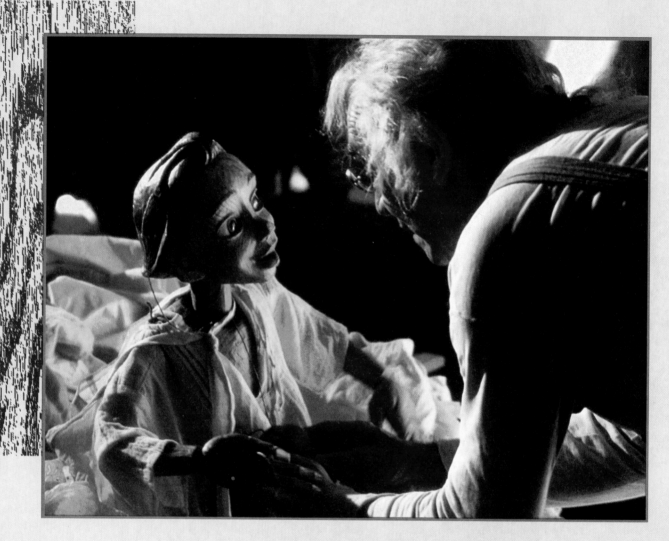

But this puppet was not like the others. He did not need
strings to walk.

"Papa!" said the puppet.

Geppetto gasped. Was he losing his mind?

"Pinocchio," he said firmly. "You're a *puppet*, not a real boy."

"Real boy!" Pinocchio insisted.

Word spread. Soon the whole town knew that Geppetto had made a new puppet, one that needed no strings. Lorenzini appeared at Geppetto's door. He hoped to buy Pinocchio and put him on the stage. But Geppetto loved Pinocchio, loved him as he would a son.

"He's not for sale," he said.

Lorenzini eyed Pinocchio. He wanted the puppet badly.

As the men talked, Pinocchio slipped out the door. He fell in line with some boys, and followed them to school. One of the boys hit Pinocchio. Pinocchio struck back.

"Did you do that?" asked the schoolmaster.

"No," lied Pinocchio.

Suddenly, Pinocchio's nose started to grow. The more he lied, the longer it grew!

"Out!" cried the schoolmaster. "Get out of my school!"

Pinocchio wandered through the piazza and came to a
bakery. The pastries looked inviting. Pinocchio dipped his
finger into a dab of icing. It was delicious! Soon, he had
eaten half the pastries in the shop. The baker's wife shrieked
when she saw what he had done.

Geppetto rushed in, looking for Pinocchio.

"Arrest them!" cried the baker's wife.

The police grabbed Geppetto and hauled him off to jail. Pinocchio slipped from their grasp.

That night, Pinocchio sat alone in Geppetto's house. He stared at the dying embers of the fire. Suddenly, someone spoke to him. It was a small cricket named Pepe. Pepe had come to teach Pinocchio the difference between right and wrong. A knock sounded at the door.

"Answer it," Pepe instructed.

It was the police. They caught Pinocchio by his thin, wooden arms and carried the poor puppet away.

Geppetto and Pinocchio were called before the court.

"You must pay the baker," the magistrate told Geppetto. "If you cannot, you will go to debtor's prison."

Geppetto had no money. He was only a poor woodsman. If he went to prison, who would care for his curious little puppet?

Lorenzini stepped up to the magistrate.

"I will pay," he volunteered. "But in return, I will keep Pinocchio."

Pinocchio reached for Geppetto. "Papa!" he cried.

Lorenzini took Pinocchio in his arms and carried him out of the courtroom.

At Lorenzini's theater, Pinocchio took the part of the hero. He had to kill the great Colossus and save the princess. The audience applauded wildly. After the scene, Lorenzini dropped five gold coins into Pinocchio's hand.

"I love being a star!" cried Pinocchio.

"Hurry," urged Lorenzini. "Go out and finish the show."

Then Lorenzini wheeled a sea monster onto the stage.
The monster breathed flames, burning the puppets. This was
not acting, it was real!

"My papa made those puppets!" cried Pinocchio.

He pulled the princess from the fire. The flames leaped to
the sail of a ship. Soon, the whole stage was aflame.
Everyone ran for their lives.

Pinocchio ran out of the theater. He jumped into the river and drifted far from town. Finally, he climbed ashore in the forest, settling against the stump of an old tree. Pepe perched on the puppet's nose.

"You can't stay here and sleep your problems away," the cricket advised. "You've got to get back to your papa."

Geppetto was, indeed, very worried about Pinocchio. He'd searched for him everywhere. Geppetto's friend Leona searched, as well.

"He's probably gone to the woods," she said. "The woods are his home. He'll feel safe there."

The two set off to comb the forest.

Two thieves were wandering in the forest. They were
Felinet and Volpe, friends of Lorenzini's. When they came
upon Pinocchio, they knew his pocket was bulging with gold.

"You should plant your coins," they said, to trick him.
"The coins will grow into more."

The thieves led Pinocchio away, then stole back and dug
up the riches themselves.

Pinocchio continued down the road. He came upon Lampwick, one of the boys he had met at school. Lampwick and his friends were riding to Terra Magica, a special playland for boys. Pinocchio jumped aboard.

Geppetto's cart drove past. "Look!" he cried to Leona. "There's Pinocchio!" Geppetto turned his cart around and snapped the reins, hurrying to catch up.

Terra Magica was a boy's paradise. There were pillow fights and fireworks, tugs-of-war and big bowls of creepy-crawly bugs. In Terra Magica, there were no bedtimes, no parents, no schoolmasters, no rules!

Pepe had followed Pinocchio to the playland. He watched as Pinocchio got into one sort of mischief after another.

"Go back to Geppetto," he urged. "Or do you have a wooden heart as well as a wooden head?"

But Pinocchio was having too much fun. He ran off with Lampwick. There were more thrills, more games to play!

20

Geppetto continued to search for Pinocchio. The road he had followed ended. Before him stretched the vast, churning sea. Maybe Pinocchio was out there. The wizened old woodsman climbed into a boat. He was determined to find his little wooden son.

In Terra Magica, the boys grew wilder and wilder. They boarded a ride called "The Big One." Their cart inched up a steep track. *Zoom!* It sped down a hill and tore around a curve. It splashed through a fountain. The boys opened their mouths wide and gulped the water thirstily.

Suddenly, Lampwick's face began to change. His nose grew into a donkey's snout! The water in the fountain was enchanted! The other boys grew donkey tails! Even Pinocchio sprouted long, wooden donkey ears.

"I don't want to be a donkey," moaned Pinocchio.

"You should have thought of that before you started acting like one," Pepe told him.

As the cart rolled to a stop, Lorenzini greeted the boys.
"Get that puppet!" he cried, when he spied Pinocchio.
Lampwick reared. *Splash!* Lorenzini fell backward, into the
enchanted fountain. As the boys watched, the greedy
showman turned into a scaly green sea monster. He scrambled
over the rocks and fell off the edge of a cliff, into the swirling
river below.

Pinocchio and Lampwick left Terra Magica behind and set off in search of Geppetto. They came upon Leona.

"Where's my papa?" Pinocchio asked.

Leona pointed out to sea. Pinocchio jumped into a small boat and rowed it into the pounding surf.

25

Soon, Pinocchio's boat started to pitch and roll. It wasn't waves that tossed him. Pinocchio had rowed onto the back of a large sea monster. It was Lorenzini! The monster opened his huge, cavernous mouth. Pinocchio washed past the monster's teeth and slid into the dark, slimy pit of his stomach.

"Ahoy, Captain!" cried Pepe. Pepe was there! Pinocchio tucked the little cricket into his pocket. Then Pinocchio came upon Geppetto. He had been swallowed by the monster, as well!

"Come on!" cried Geppetto. "Let's find a way out of here!"

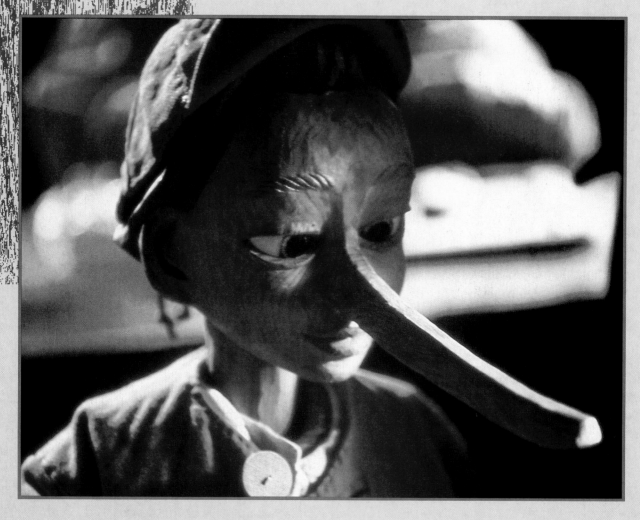

Pinocchio and Geppetto hiked up the throat of the monster. The throat grew narrow, too narrow for them to squeeze through. Pinocchio had an idea.

"I hate you, Papa!" he cried. Pinocchio's nose started to grow. "I *never, ever* missed you," he said louder.

His nose grew even longer.

Pinocchio's nose pushed against the monster's throat. *Snap!* His nose broke off, prying the mouth open. Pinocchio and Geppetto scrambled out. The sea monster thrashed, unable to close his mouth against the water rushing in. He sank to the bottom of the cold, murky sea.

Pinocchio and Geppetto struggled through the waves. Finally, they washed up on shore. Pinocchio wiped the sand from his father's cheek.

"I'm sorry, Papa," he said, "for not being a real boy."

"You're real to me, my son," said Geppetto. "I love you."

Pinocchio started to cry. The tears were real, not wooden. His tears fell upon the heart that Geppetto had carved in his chest. They softened the wood. The heart began to throb.

"Pinocchio!" gasped Geppetto. Before his eyes, the wooden boy was turning to flesh.

"I'm a real boy!" cried Pinocchio, waving his arms and kicking his strong, new legs.

Leona helped Geppetto into his cart. The three drove off. They were a family now. The cart trundled down the road, headed for home.

And so, each day, Pinocchio grew, as real boys will. Lampwick had become a boy again as well. Geppetto watched as the two friends ran off. "Boys will be boys," he said, smiling.

Geppetto was happy. His home now rang with the cheerful sounds of laughter and play. Now, at last, he had a child, a real child, not wooden, a son of flesh and blood. Geppetto had the child he'd always wanted.